ICE SKATES

SKIS

POLES

ICICLES

SNOW-ANGEL

SNOW CATS

ANDY

For my "SNOW" friend, Carol Morrissey Greiner
—T. deP.

For Linda, Leo, "The Brow," and all the Chestnut Street sleigh riders
—J. L.

SIMON & SCHUSTER BOOKS FOR YOUNG READERS
An imprint of Simon & Schuster Children's Publishing Division
1230 Avenue of the Americas, New York, New York 10020
Text copyright © 2016 by Tomie dePaola and Jim Lewis
Illustrations copyright © 2016 by Tomie dePaola
SIMON & SCHUSTER BOOKS FOR YOUNG READERS is a trademark of Simon & Schuster, Inc.
For information about special discounts for bulk purchases, please contact
Simon & Schuster Special Sales at 1-866-506-1949 or business@simonandschuster.com.
The Simon & Schuster Speakers Bureau can bring authors to your live event.
For more information or to book an event, contact the Simon & Schuster Speakers Bureau
at 1-866-248-3049 or visit our website at www.simonspeakers.com.
Book design by Laurent Linn
The text for this book was set in Minister Std.
The illustrations for this book were rendered in acrylics with colored pencil
on 150lb Fabriano Cold Press 100% rag watercolor paper.
Manufactured in China
0716 SCP
First Edition
2 4 6 8 10 9 7 5 3 1
CIP data for this book is available from the Library of Congress.
ISBN 978-1-4814-4159-9
ISBN 978-1-4814-4160-5 (eBook)

Andy & Sandy and the First Snow

Tomie dePaola
COWRITTEN WITH Jim Lewis

SIMON & SCHUSTER BOOKS FOR YOUNG READERS
New York   London   Toronto   Sydney   New Delhi

Hooray! The first snow of winter!

Snow is very wet
and VERY COLD.

But snow is lots of fun!
Follow me.

You roll a
small snowball.

I'll roll a bigger
snowball.

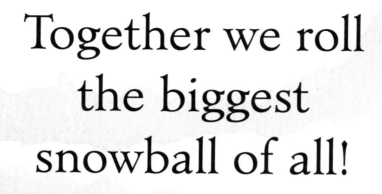

Together we roll
the biggest
snowball of all!

He looks
cold.

He needs a hat
and scarf.

Our snowman!

Where are we going now?

Up the hill!

The sled is not going.

I can help!

Whee!

Now what?

In the snow?

Fall down!

Now flap your arms and legs. Like this!

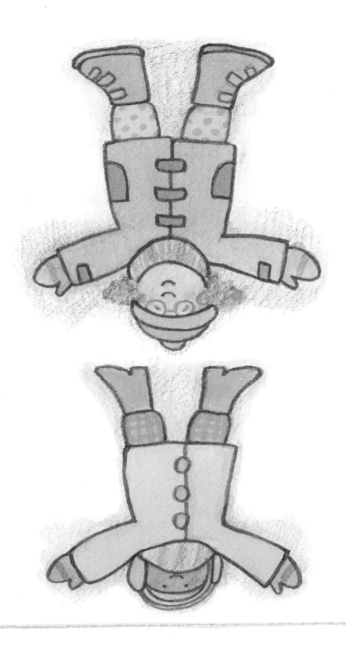

Snow angels!

Snow is very wet
and very cold.

And snow is lots of fun!

But the best part is getting warm.